WITHDRAWN

The Little Forest Keepers

By Mary Lundquist

Balzer + Bray
An Imprint of HarperCollinsPublishers

Balzer + Bray
is an imprint of HarperCollins Publishers.

The Little Forest Keepers
Copyright © 2021 by Mary Lundquist
All rights reserved. Manufactured in Italy.
No part of this book may be used or reproduced in any manner whatsoever without written permission
except in the case of brief quotations embodied in critical articles and reviews. For information address
HarperCollins Children's Books, a division of HarperCollins Publishers, 195 Broadway, New York, NY 10007.
www.harpercollinschildrens.com

ISBN 978-0-06-228782-3

The artist used watercolor, gouache and pencil on watercolor paper to create the illustrations for this book.
Typography by Dana Fritts
21 22 23 24 25   RTLO   10 9 8 7 6 5 4 3 2 1
❖

For my mother-in-law, Sherry.
Thank you for keeping our little forest
of a family together. You keep us warm
and cozy and always well fed.
With love, Mary

Ash and Pudd woke up extra early.
"Let's go, Pudd!"

It was going to snow, and
they had a lot of work to do.

The brothers loaded their sled and set out.

Ash and Pudd took care of everyone in the forest.

They knitted hats and scarves for
the animals and fed them nuts and
seeds and berries.

"Bundle up, everyone!"

The little forest keepers even took care
of the shivering trees.

It was very important work.

That day, the boys saw something new
and strange peeking up from over the hill.

"Ash, what could it be?"

They had never seen anything like this before.

So they decided to climb it.

Up and up they went . . .

until they finally reached the top. From there they could see the forest all around them. But when they leaned over to look down—

Whoops!

The thing had a face!
"Hurry, Pudd!"

They ran away as quickly as they could.
When they turned around to look at it,
though, the strange new thing didn't look
so scary anymore.

It looked lonely.

The snow was falling hard as the boys returned home. They were glad all their friends had scarves and hats to keep them cozy and warm.

But they kept thinking about the big lonely thing at the edge of the forest. Suddenly, Pudd had an idea.

"More yarn, Ash!"

In the morning, Ash and Pudd set out
again, this time with some help.

Again they went up and up and up

to finish their important work.

It was Ash and Pudd's job to take care
of everyone in the woods,

friends both old and new.
And that's exactly what they did.